What Riley Wore

Written by Elana K. Arnold Illustrated by Linda Davick

Beach Lane Books • New York   London   Toronto   Sydney   New Delhi

BEACH LANE BOOKS

An imprint of Simon & Schuster Children's Publishing Division

1230 Avenue of the Americas, New York, New York 10020

Text copyright © 2019 by Elana K. Arnold

Illustrations copyright © 2019 by Linda Davick

BEACH LANE BOOKS is a trademark of Simon & Schuster, Inc.

For information about special discounts for bulk purchases, please contact Simon & Schuster Special Sales at
1-866-506-1949 or business@simonandschuster.com.

The Simon & Schuster Speakers Bureau can bring authors to your live event. For more information or to book an event,
contact the Simon & Schuster Speakers Bureau at 1-866-248-3049 or visit our website at www.simonspeakers.com.

Book design by Lauren Rille

The text for this book was set in Write.

The illustrations for this book were rendered digitally.

Manufactured in China

0619 SCP

First Edition

10 9 8 7 6 5 4 3 2 1

Library of Congress Cataloging-in-Publication Data

Names: Arnold, Elana K., author. | Davick, Linda, illustrator.

Title: What Riley wore / Elana K. Arnold ; illustrated by Linda Davick.

Description: First edition. | New York : Beach Lane Books, [2019] | Summary: "Gender-creative Riley knows just what to
wear for every occasion during a busy week with family and friends"— Provided by publisher.

Identifiers: LCCN 2017054336 | ISBN 9781481472609 (hardcover : alk. paper) | ISBN 9781481472616 (ebook)

Subjects: | CYAC: Clothing and dress—Fiction. | Gender identity—Fiction. | Friendship—Fiction. | Family life—Fiction.

Classification: LCC PZ7.A73517 Whl 2018 | DDC [E—dc23 LC record available at https://lccn.loc.gov/2017054336

For all the Rileys,
with love
—E. K. A.

For Jamie, who loved
to borrow my green jumpsuit
—L. D.

On Monday, Riley wore a bunny costume

because it was the first day of school and Riley felt shy.

It was true that no one else in class wore a bunny costume.

But it was also true that a girl who was crying asked
if she could touch one of the ears.

Riley said, "Yes!

The ears feel just like real velvet."

On Tuesday, Riley wore a superhero cape to the dentist's office because teeth cleaning is scary and Riley wanted to be brave. The dentist asked,

"What's your superpower?"

Riley said,

"I'll have to get back to you on that."

On Wednesday, Riley wore a ball gown out to dinner with Otto and Oma because they went to a fancy restaurant, and ball gowns are the fanciest.

When Riley spilled tomato soup,
Oma used ginger ale to blot it out.

A kid at another table said they should leave
the stain just as it was because it looked
like a star and stars are cool.

Thursday was Universe Day at school,
so Riley decided that outer space jammies
were the perfect thing to wear.

Riley's teacher loved the jammies, and he asked Riley to stand on a chair while he pointed out the planets on Riley's back. Then everyone used scissors and glue and construction paper and made planets of their own.

It rained on Friday, so Riley wore a colorful combination of rubber boots, a police officer jacket, and the world's best tutu.

The crossing guard told Riley, "I had a pair of rain boots just like that when I was little."

The recess captain, a big kid in the sixth grade, told Riley, "I like your tutu."

When the weather turned mild on Saturday,
Riley dressed in a hard hat and overalls to help
Dad run errands.

Three guys at the hardware store called Riley

"Daddy's Little Helper," and one of them gave Riley a sticker.

Riley didn't peel it away from its backing because

maybe it would make a good present for a friend someday.

When they got home, Riley tucked the sticker away for safekeeping and wondered if being a friend could be a superpower.

Sunday was a lazy home day.

Riley spent part of it wearing nothing at all.

But when Mom asked

who wanted to go to the park,

Riley put on one striped sock . . .

and one polka-dot sock . . .

purple jeans,

the world's best tutu,

a crazy monster shirt,

red rubber boots,

round aviator goggles,

and a hat with dinosaur spikes.

At the park, Riley felt shy.

Then a kid from school

walked up and asked,

"Are you a girl or a boy?"

Riley said,

"Today I'm a firefighter.

And a dancer.

And a monster hunter.

And a pilot.

And a dinosaur."

"Oh," said the kid.

"Want to play?"

"Yes!" Then Riley reached into a pocket, pulled out the sticker, and gave it to the kid.

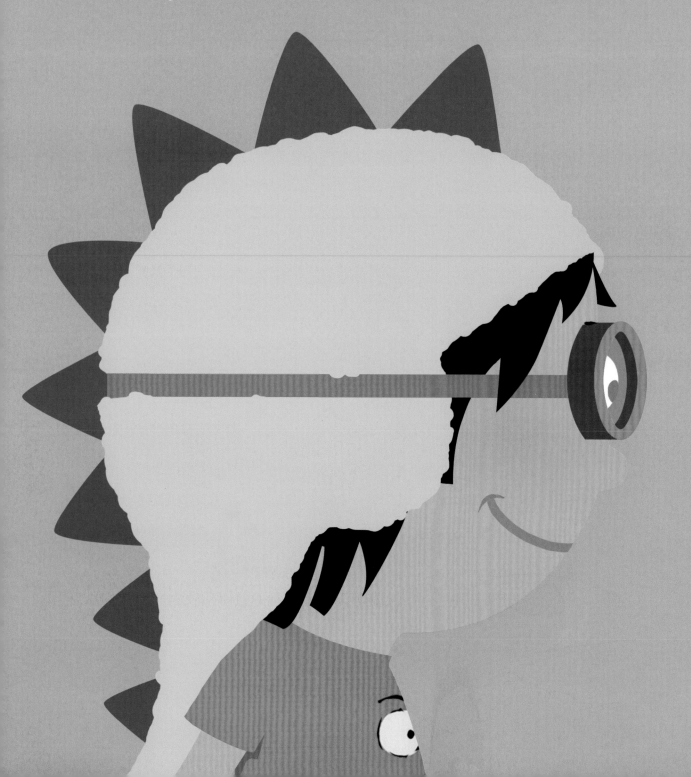

The kid smiled.

And Riley felt wonderful.